Dear Parent:
Your child's love of reading starts here!

Every child learns to read in a different way and at his or her own speed. Some go back and forth between reading levels and read favorite books again and again. Others read through each level in order. You can help your young reader improve and become more confident by encouraging his or her own interests and abilities. From books your child reads with you to the first books he or she reads alone, there are I Can Read Books for every stage of reading:

SHARED READING
Basic language, word repetition, and whimsical illustrations, ideal for sharing with your emergent reader

BEGINNING READING
Short sentences, familiar words, and simple concepts for children eager to read on their own

READING WITH HELP
Engaging stories, longer sentences, and language play for developing readers

READING ALONE
Complex plots, challenging vocabulary, and high-interest topics for the independent reader

ADVANCED READING
Short paragraphs, chapters, and exciting themes for the perfect bridge to chapter books

I Can Read Books have introduced children to the joy of reading since 1957. Featuring award-winning authors and illustrators and a fabulous cast of beloved characters, I Can Read Books set the standard for beginning readers.

A lifetime of discovery begins with the magical words "I Can Read!"

Visit www.icanread.com for information on enriching your child's reading experience.

For Peter and Laura,
who love to go camping
under the stars!
—A.S.C.

I Can Read Book® is a trademark of HarperCollins Publishers.

ISBN 978-0-06-223693-7 (pbk.) — ISBN 978-0-06-223694-4 (trade bdg.)

The artist used traditional watercolor and Photoshop to create the digital illustrations for this book.

15 16 17 18 19   SCP   10 9 8 7 6 5 4 3 2 1   ❖   First Edition

Biscuit Goes Camping

story by ALYSSA SATIN CAPUCILLI
pictures by PAT SCHORIES

HARPER
An Imprint of HarperCollins Publishers

This way, Biscuit.

It's time to go camping.

Woof, woof!

We have our tent.

Woof!

We have our flashlight
and blankets, too.
Woof, woof!

Silly puppy!
No tugging.

6

It's time to go camping.
Woof!

Wait, Biscuit.

What have you found?

Woof, woof!

Croak!

You found a frog, Biscuit.

Woof, woof!

Whoo-oo! Whoo-oo!

Funny puppy.

It's only the wind, Biscuit.

There are so many
new sights and sounds
when you go camping.
Woof!

Oh, Biscuit!

What have you found now?

Woof, woof!

Blink! Blink!
It's a firefly, Biscuit.
The firefly says
good night.

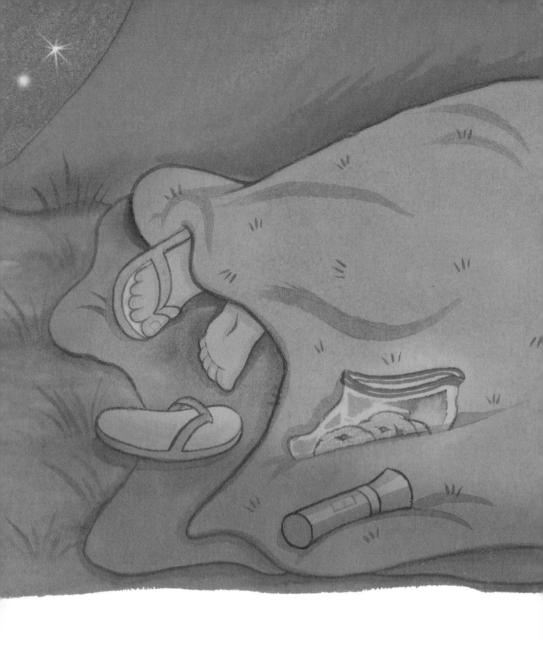

It's time for us to say
good night, too, Biscuit.

Curl up, Biscuit.

Woof, woof!

Crack! Crack!

Boom! Boom!

Oh no!

Here comes the rain!

How can we go camping now?

Woof, woof!

Woof, woof!

Biscuit! Wait for me!

Woof!

Smart puppy!

You found the perfect

place to go camping.

Blink! Blink!

Woof, woof!

Good night, Biscuit.